DATE DUE

OCT 14	OCT 31		
OCT 20	NOV 10		
OCT 23	NOV 15		
NOV 20	DEC 1		
	DEC 6		
NOV 30			
DEC 14	DEC 20		
DEC 16	JAN 3		
DEC 22	JAN 17		
JAN 20	JAN 19		
JAN 28	JAN 31		
FEB 8	FEB 8		
	FEB 16		
FEB 10			
FEB 25	MAR 9		
MAR 24	APR 17		
APR 5	NOV 10		
APR 8	MAY 4		
MAY 18			
MAY 25			
MAY 25			

170 IDEAL   PRINTED IN U.S.A.

EASY TO READ BOOKS
BY SARAH DERMAN

PRETTY BIRD
SURPRISE EGG
PONY RING
BIG TOP
MONKEY ISLAND
POKER DOG

pictures

by Jack Boyd

Benefic Press · Chicago

Publishing division of Beckley-Cardy Company

POKER DOG

By

Sarah Derman

STORIES

Poker's Friends

Every one knew Poker.
And Poker knew every one.
Poker was a brown and white dog.
He had ears that came way down.
And he had a poker nose
that looked for good things to eat.

Every one knew
Poker liked to eat.
Every one knew
he liked children.
Poker had fun
with the children
every day.

But there was one
thing no one knew.
No one knew
where Poker lived.
The policeman
thought he was
the postman's dog.
Poker went
with the postman
every day.

The postman thought he was
the fireman's dog.
Poker had friends at the fire house.
He went to see them.
His friends put something on him.

The fireman
thought Poker was
the children's dog.
Poker liked to go
with the children.

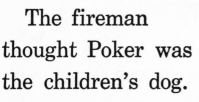

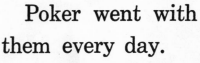

Poker went with
them every day.
All the children
liked Poker.
But Poker did not
go home with them.

When it was day,
Poker had fun.

He jumped in the leaves.

He saw all his friends.

He ran and jumped with them.

But when night came, no one
ran and jumped with him.

Poker did not have fun
at night.

Every one went
home at night.
Poker did not
know where to go.
Poker did not
have a home.
Poker was
no one's dog.

Miss Pearl's Garden

Miss Pearl sat in her chair
and looked at her garden.
No one lived with Miss Pearl.
Poker wanted to be Miss Pearl's dog.
Miss Pearl did not know this.

One night it was cold.

Poker went into Miss Pearl's
garden to sleep.

He put his poker nose
into the leaves.

That night Poker went to sleep
in Miss Pearl's garden.

When day came, Miss Pearl went
to work in her garden.

She took something into her garden.
It was something to work with.

Miss Pearl wanted her garden
to be pretty.

Then Miss Pearl saw something.
She did not like what she saw.
She saw a big hole!
Miss Pearl did not want holes
in her garden.
Her garden could not be pretty
with holes in it.

Miss Pearl looked all around.
"Who made this hole?" she said.

"I want to see
who is in my
garden," Miss Pearl
said then.

"I do not like
big holes in my
garden. Big holes
are not pretty."

Miss Pearl looked in the leaves.
She saw Poker's nose.
There was Poker sleeping
in the leaves.
"This is the one who is
in my garden," said Miss Pearl.
"Now I know who made
the hole."
She said to Poker,
"You made that
big hole.
Now get out!"

Poker Gets Hurt

Poker jumped up.

Up and down the garden ran Poker.

Up and down the garden ran Miss Pearl after Poker.

Around and around the garden they went.

They ran and ran.

But Poker did not look where
he was running.

There was something in Poker's way.

It was something Miss Pearl had
for her garden.

She worked with it.

Poker did not know that there
was something in his way.

Down went Poker!

Poker was hurt, and he cried.

Poker had hurt his paw.

He looked at his paw, and then he looked around.

Poker could not run now.

He saw Miss Pearl!

Poker wanted her to know that he had hurt his paw.

Miss Pearl saw him.

Miss Pearl stopped.
Then she saw
Poker cry.

She did not like
holes in her garden.

But Miss Pearl
did not want
a dog to be hurt.

Miss Pearl went
to Poker.

Miss Pearl looked at Poker's paw.

"There, there," she said.

"Your paw is hurt.

But soon it will be all right.

We will get some one

to look after it."

At the Hospital

Poker went with Miss Pearl.
Soon they came to a big white house.
On the house it said,
      HOSPITAL FOR DOGS.

A man in white came out.
Miss Pearl said,
"This dog has
hurt his paw.
Will you
look at it?"

"Come in," said
the man. "We will
take your dog."

Into the hospital went Poker.
The man in white
took Poker.
He looked
at Poker's paw.

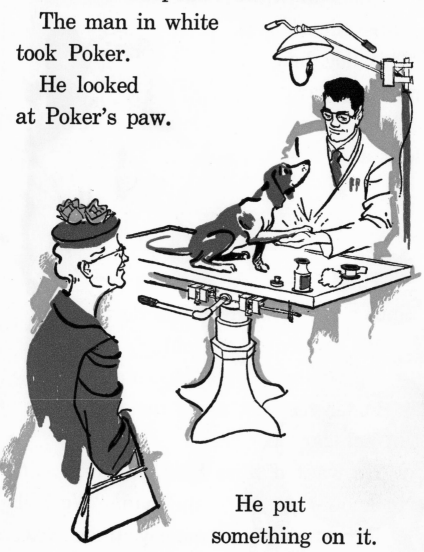

He put
something on it.

Then Poker was put
into a little room with a door.
He wanted to get out.
He wanted to see Miss Pearl.
Poker had not made the hole
in her garden.
He wanted Miss Pearl
to know that.
But Miss Pearl was not there now.

Then Poker looked around.
He saw many, many dogs.
They were in little rooms, too.
There were big dogs and little dogs.
There were black dogs, and
there were white dogs.

Some dogs had tails, and some had
no tails at all.

There was one big dog
with some very little dogs.

The very little dogs could not see.
But oh, how they liked to eat!

The Dogs Get Baths

The dogs were going to take baths.
The man in white had some
of the dogs go into the bath room.
The dogs looked and looked.
The dogs
did not know
what the man
was going to do.

All the dogs had baths.
Some did not like
their baths.

One little dog
took something.
A man in white
ran after him.

After they had their baths,
the dogs were put into little rooms
to dry.

When the dogs came out
of the little rooms, they were dry.

Now the dogs wanted to eat.

The man in white had dinners
for all the dogs.

Some of the dogs sat up
for their dinners.

Poker sat up
for his dinner, too.

The man in white
put the dinners
in the little rooms.
There were little
dinners for the
little dogs.
And there were big dinners
for the big dogs.

After the big dogs
had their dinners,
they looked around.

They looked at the little dogs
and their dinners.

The big dogs wanted
to eat the little dinners, too.

After he had his dinner,
Poker wanted to sleep.

That night Poker did not have
to look in the leaves.

He knew where he was going
to sleep.

He went to sleep in his room
at the dog hospital.

Suzy And Pug

Poker looked out his door.
He saw a pretty little dog
in one of the rooms.
The pretty little dog cried
and cried.

The man in white said, "Suzy,
you look pretty.

Now you can be in the dog show."

But Suzy cried and cried.

She did not want to look pretty
for the dog show.

She wanted to go home.

Then a big girl came to see Suzy.

"I will come to get you soon, Suzy," said the girl.

Suzy looked at the girl.

She did not cry when the big girl was with her.

Suzy knew she could go home soon with the big girl.

No one came to see Poker.
No one said, "I will take you
home when your paw is all right."
Poker did not have a home.
Then Poker saw Pug.

Pug was a big farm dog.
Pug had hurt his ear
in a dog fight.

He put his nose up to his door.
He saw Suzy cry.

Pug did not like the hospital,
but he did not cry.

He did not want Suzy to cry.

But Suzy wanted the big girl
to come.

Soon a man came to get Pug.
"Come, Pug," said the man.

"We will go home now.

But you can not fight."

Pug looked down.
He did not look at the man.

Pug was not going to fight.

In a very little box was a very,
very little dog.

This dog was Twigs.

A little girl came to the door.

The little girl wanted to take
her little dog home.

Twigs wanted to go home with her.

Twigs had fun with the little girl.

He did not like the hospital.

The man
in white gave
Twigs to the
little girl.

Then he
said, "Twigs
still has a
little cold.

But it is all right for him
to go home with you."

The little girl
did not want Twigs
to be cold.

She did not put
him in a little box.

Twigs liked to go
with the girl.

It was fun.

Where To Go?

Now all the dogs were home.
No one was at the hospital
with Poker.

Poker looked at all the little rooms.
No one was there.

The man in white came in.

"How is your paw?" he said.

The man looked at Poker's paw.

"It is all right for you to go home now, too," the man in white said.

"Your paw will not hurt now."

But Poker did not know
where to go.

Poker looked
around at the
little rooms.

Suzy was not there.
By now, she was
in a dog show.

By now, Pug
was on the farm.

Twigs was not there.
The little girl
put him in a box
at home.

Poker had no home to think about.
He thought about Miss Pearl.
He thought about her garden, too.

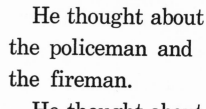

He thought about
the policeman and
the fireman.

He thought about
going around with
the postman.

But he did not
know something.

Poker's friends
were thinking
about him, too.

That day Miss
Pearl went to look
at her garden.

Then Miss Pearl
saw something.

She did not like
what she saw.

Holes!

There were holes
all around in her
pretty garden.

Now Miss Pearl did not know
what to think.

Poker could not have made
all the holes.

He was in the hospital.

Miss Pearl looked.
She saw some
big ears.

Miss Pearl ran
after the big ears.
She ran up and
down the garden.

But the big ears
went down a hole.
Miss Pearl could
not see them.

Then Miss Pearl
sat down to think.
She said, "I do
not want rabbits
in my garden."
Now Miss Pearl
thought of Poker.

Miss Pearl said,
"I need a dog
to look after
my garden.
I need a dog
to be my friend."
Then Miss Pearl
ran to the
dog hospital.

Poker's Friends Come

But on the way to the hospital,
Miss Pearl saw some one.

There was the fireman going
to the hospital.

"I want Poker for my dog," he said.

"He can sleep in the fire house."

When she came to the hospital,
there was the postman.

"Did you know Poker was hurt?"
said the postman.

"I will take him home with me.
He will be a good dog for me."

Now Miss Pearl did not think she
was going to get Poker for her dog.

The fireman had a home for Poker.

The postman had a home
for him, too.

They all went into the hospital
to see Poker.

The policeman was at the hospital.
He was with the man in white.
"We have a big barn at our house,"
the policeman said to him.
"Poker could sleep in the barn.

I want to take
Poker with me.
He could be
a good dog
for a policeman."
Now the
policeman wanted
Poker, too.

Then the man in white looked
at Miss Pearl.

"I need a dog," said Miss Pearl.
"No one lives with me.
I need a dog to be my friend.
I need a dog to run
after the rabbits
in my garden."

"Oh, oh," said the man in white.
"Now we have too many homes.
Poker could be the fireman's dog
and sleep at the fire house.
He could be the policeman's dog
and sleep
in the barn."

Then he said,
"Poker could be
the postman's dog
and go around with him every day."

"Poker could be Miss Pearl's friend," said the man in white.

"He could run after the rabbits in her garden."

Then he looked at Miss Pearl, the policeman, the postman, and the fireman.

"Who knows what to do?" he said.

Poker Gets A Home

Poker jumped.
Then he ran around Miss Pearl.
Poker wanted
them to know
that he liked
Miss Pearl.

The man in white knew then that
Poker wanted to be Miss Pearl's dog.

"Miss Pearl needs Poker.

And Poker needs Miss Pearl,"
said the man in white.

Then the man in white said that
Poker could go home with Miss Pearl.

Now Poker was Miss Pearl's dog.

Now Poker had a home.

Every one liked that.

Now Poker runs after
all the rabbits in Miss
Pearl's garden.

He still sees the
policeman and goes
with the postman.

He still goes to the
fire house, too.

But when night comes
Poker knows where he
is going to sleep.

He sleeps right in Miss Pearl's big chair!

VOCABULARY

The total number of different words used in this book is one hundred forty-seven, excluding proper names. Of these, thirty are first-grade level or above. These words and the numbers of the pages on which they first appear are listed below. The five words shown in italics are above first-grade level. The remaining one hundred seventeen words are below first-grade level.

baths   30

children   6
cold   13
cried   20
cry   22

ears   5

fight   41
fire   8
fireman   9
friend(s)   5

garden   12

hole(s)   15
hospital   24
hurt   18

knew   5

leaves   13

many   28

need(s)   52
nose   5

paw   20
policeman   7
poker   5
postman   7

room(s)   27
running   19

show   38
sleeping   17

their   31
think   48
thought   7